THIS CANDLEWICK BOOK BELONGS TO:

_____

_____

_____

The Nightingale

CANDLEWICK PRESS
CAMBRIDGE, MASSACHUSETTS

HANS CHRISTIAN ANDERSEN
The Nightingale

retold by Stephen Mitchell

illustrated by
Bagram Ibatoulline

To Mayo and Shelton Chang and to Daniel Chang

S. M.

To my wife, Olga, my son, Anton, and all good friends

B. I.

In China, as you know, the Emperor is Chinese, and all the people are Chinese, too. The story you're about to hear happened a long time ago, but even after all this time it hasn't been forgotten, and that's why I can tell it to you now.

The Emperor lived in the most marvelous palace in the world. It was made completely of porcelain, just like fine cups and saucers. All the walls and floors and tables and chairs were porcelain, and they were so thin and breakable that you had to be extra-specially careful when you touched them.

The Emperor's garden was filled with the rarest and most beautiful flowers. Each one had a little silver bell tied to it. Whenever you walked past a flower, its bell would tinkle so that you'd be sure to notice it.

The garden stretched out so far and so wide that even the Chief Imperial Gardener had no idea where it ended. If you kept on walking past the flower beds, you finally came to a magnificent forest, with tall trees and clear lakes. The forest stretched all the way to the sea, which was deep enough so that large ships could sail right in under the branches of the trees.

In this forest near the seashore there lived a nightingale. Her song was so lovely that even the fisherman, who was busy pulling in his nets in the moonlight, would stop and listen to her. He looked up into the treetops, and a smile lit up his face. "Ah, how beautiful that is!" he said to himself. But then he had to get back to his work, and he stopped listening.

But the next night, when the nightingale sang again, he listened again and said to himself, "Ah, how beautiful!"

From every country in the world, travelers came to China, and they went "Ooh!" and they went "Ahh!" at the Emperor's great city and at his palace and at his garden. But as soon as they heard the nightingale, they all said the same thing: "That is the loveliest of all."

And when they returned home from their travels, they had many stories to tell, and the cleverest among them wrote many books about the city and the palace and the garden, and about how magnificent they were. But they always saved the nightingale for last, because she was the loveliest of all. And all the poems that the poets wrote were about the nightingale in the forest by the sea.

These books made their way through the whole world, and in time some of them reached the Emperor. There he sat on his golden throne, reading and reading. Now and then he smiled and nodded his head. He was very pleased that everyone admired him so much and had such wonderful things to say about his city and his palace and his garden.

And then he read: "But the nightingale is the loveliest of all."

"Hmpf!" thought the Emperor. "*What* nightingale? Nobody ever told *me* about a nightingale! Is it possible that I have a nightingale in my Empire, in my very own garden, and nobody has ever mentioned it to me, and I had to discover it from a *book*?"

And immediately he summoned his Chief Imperial Gentleman-in-Waiting. Now the Chief Imperial Gentleman-in-Waiting was so exalted a person that, if anyone of a lower rank asked him a question, he wouldn't even answer with a word. "Ppp!" he would say—and that means nothing at all.

"It says here," said the Emperor, pointing to a page in the book, "that I have a most remarkable bird called a nightingale. She is a most extraordinary bird, it says, and the loveliest thing in all my Empire. Why haven't I been told about this?"

"It's the first time *I've* ever heard of her, Your Majesty," said the Gentleman-in-Waiting. "She has never been presented at Court."

"I *command* you to bring her here to sing for me this very evening!" said the Emperor. "Hmpf! The whole world knows about this remarkable bird of mine—except me!"

"It's the first time *I've* ever heard of her," repeated the Gentleman-in-Waiting. "I will look for her, Your Majesty, and I will find her."

Find her? But how?

The Gentleman-in-Waiting ran upstairs and downstairs, through rooms and corridors, but no one he met had ever heard of the nightingale. So he hurried back to the Emperor and said it must be a story made up by the clever people who write books. "You shouldn't believe everything you read, Your Majesty. Writers like to tell fairy tales, you know; they'll just make something up and not care whether it's true or not."

"But this book," said the Emperor, "was sent to me by the Emperor of Japan, and Emperors don't tell lies. Now just you listen to me. I want the nightingale here. I want her *tonight!* And if she doesn't appear after dinner at seven o'clock on the dot, every courtier in the palace will get one punch in the stomach."

"Tsing-pe!" said the Gentleman-in-Waiting, and he ran up and down all the stairs again, through all the rooms and corridors. And half the courtiers ran with him, since they weren't particularly fond of being punched in the stomach. There they all were, trying to find out about this extraordinary nightingale that everyone in the world had heard of—everyone, that is, except the people at Court.

At last they ran into a poor little girl in the palace kitchen, who said, "The nightingale? *I* know her. She sings so beautifully. I hear her every evening when I visit my poor sick mother, who lives down by the shore. I'm allowed to take my mother a few scraps from the table, and on my way back I stop for a while in the forest and listen to the nightingale's song. It brings tears to my eyes, and I feel as if my mother were well again and held me in her arms."

"Little kitchen maid," said the Gentleman-in-Waiting, "you will be promoted and you will be allowed to watch His Majesty the Emperor eat his dinner, if only you will take us to the nightingale. She has been commanded to sing at Court this very evening."

So they set out for the forest where the nightingale lived, and half the courtiers came along with them.

As they were walking, a cow began to moo. "Ah, that must be the nightingale," said the courtiers. "What a very loud song for such a small bird! But haven't we heard it somewhere before?"

"No, that's a cow mooing," said the little kitchen maid.

"Ah yes, we knew that," said the courtiers. And they kept on walking.

Then some frogs in a pond began to croak.

"Lovely!" the Chief Imperial Chamberlain said. "Just like tiny bells."

"No," said the little kitchen maid, "those are frogs. But we're getting closer." And they kept on walking.

"There she is!" cried the little kitchen maid. "There she is, way up there!" And she pointed to a small gray bird up in the branches.

"Is that really her?" said the Gentleman-in-Waiting. "How ordinary she looks! Perhaps she has lost her color because she is nervous at having so many distinguished visitors."

"Hello-o-o! *Night*ingale!" the little kitchen maid called. "The Emperor wants you to sing for him."

"With the greatest of pleasure," said the nightingale, and she sang so beautifully that it was a joy to hear.

"Just like glass bells," the Gentleman-in-Waiting said. "And look at the way her throat keeps throbbing. I can't understand why we've never heard her before. She will certainly be a great success at Court."

"Would you like me to sing another song for the Emperor?" asked the nightingale, thinking that the Emperor was there.

"Most excellent little nightingale," said the Gentleman-in-Waiting, "it is my very pleasant duty to summon you to the palace, where you will perform this evening before His Imperial Majesty the Emperor of China, and enchant him with your delightful songs."

"They really sound best in the open air," said the nightingale.

But she went along anyway, because it was the Emperor's wish.

Back at the palace, the servants had been polishing all the porcelain walls and floors and tables and chairs until they gleamed in the candlelight of a thousand golden lamps. Bouquets of the loveliest flowers lined the corridors, and what with all the doors opening and closing as the servants scurried in and out, there was such a draft that all the silver bells on the flowers kept jingling and jangling. You couldn't hear a single word that anyone said.

In the middle of the Emperor's throne room they had put a golden cage for the nightingale, with a golden perch in it. All the courtiers were there, and the little kitchen maid, who had been promoted to the rank of Imperial Servant, was allowed to stand behind the door and listen. All of them were dressed in their finest robes, and they were all looking at the small gray bird.

Finally the Emperor nodded for her to begin.

The nightingale's song was so beautiful that tears welled up in the Emperor's eyes and trickled down his cheeks. And when the nightingale saw this, her song grew even more beautiful, and pierced his heart.

The Emperor was so moved that he offered to give the nightingale his golden slipper to wear around her neck. But the nightingale said no thank you, she had already been rewarded enough. "I have seen tears of joy in the Emperor's eyes. What greater reward could there be?"

And then the nightingale sang her beautiful song again.

"What an absolutely *charming* sound!" said all the court ladies, and they went and filled their mouths with water so that they could gurgle when anyone talked to them. (They thought that this sounded like the nightingale.) Even the lackeys and the chambermaids said they were satisfied—which is saying a lot, because they were always the hardest people in the country to please.

No, there was no doubt about it: the nightingale was a great success.

She was now commanded to stay at Court, in the golden cage, with permission to go for an outing twice during the day and once at night. For these outings, twelve attendants were assigned to her. Each walked holding on to a silk ribbon tied around the nightingale's legs as she flew slightly above them. This kind of outing wasn't much fun.

Meanwhile, everyone in the city was talking about the Emperor's nightingale. Whenever two people met in the street, one would say "Nightin" and the other would say "Gale," and then they would smile and nod to each other and sigh with joy. It even went so far that eleven butchers' children were named Nightingale in her honor. (Unfortunately, all of them turned out to be tone-deaf.)

One day a package arrived for the Emperor, with the word "Nightingale" written on it.

"It's probably another book about our famous bird," said the Emperor. But it wasn't a book at all. It was a little mechanical toy, a golden nightingale that looked like a real one, except that it was covered all over with diamonds, rubies, and sapphires. All you had to do was wind it up, and it could sing one of the songs that the living nightingale sang; and as it sang, its tail flicked up and down, glittering with silver and gold. Around its neck was a ribbon, with these words: "The Emperor of Japan's nightingale is poor compared with the Emperor of China's."

"How delightful!" all the courtiers said. And the courtier who had brought in the mechanical bird was immediately given the title of Chief Imperial Nightingale Bringer.

"Now they must both sing together," somebody suggested. "What a wonderful duet that would be!"

So the two birds sang together. But it didn't turn out very well, because the real nightingale sang in her own way, while the mechanical bird's tune was as regular as the ticking of a clock. "It's not the new bird's fault," said the Chief Imperial Music Master. "*It* keeps perfect time. In fact, it sings according to my very own method."

Then the mechanical bird sang by itself. It was just as big a success as the real one, and of course it was much prettier to look at, glittering with all its jewels.

Over and over and over it sang its one tune. It sang thirty-three times in a row, and still it wasn't tired. The courtiers would have been glad to hear the song again, but the Emperor said that it was time now for the real nightingale to do a little singing.

But where *was* she?

She had flown out the open window and gone home to her green forest. And nobody had even noticed.

"How dare she leave without my permission!" the Emperor shouted, and all the courtiers scowled and said what an ungrateful creature the nightingale was.

"Anyway," they added, "the one we have is better." So the mechanical bird had to sing its one tune for the thirty-fourth time. (Nobody knew the tune by heart yet, because it was quite complicated.)

Then the Chief Imperial Music Master stood up and gave a speech in praise of the bird. He said that it was, in fact, better than the real nightingale, not only because its outside was so much more beautiful, with all its diamonds and rubies, but also because of its inner mechanism.

"You see, ladies and gentlemen, and above all, Your Imperial Majesty," the Music Master said, "when the real nightingale sings, you can never tell what's going to happen. But with the mechanical bird, everything is decided in advance. We know that one tune will be heard, and no other. We can explain the bird completely: we can open it up and examine it and see exactly how one particular screw turns one particular wheel that moves one particular hammer that makes one particular note, and everything is as clear as day."

"That's exactly what *I* think!" all the courtiers said.

Then the Music Master was given permission to show the mechanical bird to the public on the following Sunday.

"They, too, must hear it sing," said the Emperor.

And when Sunday came around, everyone heard it, and they were as happy as if they had just eaten a delicious meal. They all looked up at the bird and pointed their fingers and said, "Oh!"

But the poor fisherman who had heard the real nightingale thought, "It does sound a bit like the real one. But something is missing."

Soon an imperial edict was issued stating that the real nightingale was forever banished from the Empire.

Meanwhile, the mechanical bird had been assigned a place on a silk cushion next to the Emperor's bed. The Emperor gave it many presents of gold and jewels, and promoted it to the rank of Chief Imperial Bedside Singer of the First Class on the Left. (It was his opinion that the side which contains the heart is the more distinguished one; and an emperor, just like the rest of us, has his heart on the left side.)

The Music Master wrote a study of the mechanical bird, in twenty-five volumes. It was a very learned study and was filled with the most difficult Chinese words. All the courtiers pretended that they had read and understood it; otherwise they would have been considered stupid and gotten punched in the stomach.

Things continued like this for a whole year, until the Emperor and the courtiers and all the people knew the mechanical bird's tune backward and forward. They knew every little trill, every gurgle in its throat; and that was why they preferred it. They even joined in the singing themselves. The little ragamuffins in the street sang, "Zee-zee-zee, gloo-gloo-gloo!" and the Emperor sang it, too. It was great fun.

But one evening, while the mechanical bird was in the middle of its tune and the Emperor was lying in bed listening, something inside it went *ping!* Then there was a *whirr!* and a *clunk!* and the music stopped.

The Emperor jumped out of bed and sent for his doctor, but what could *he* do? Then they summoned the watchmaker, and after a lot of talk and poking around he got the bird to work—sort of. But he said that it had to be used very seldom, since the parts were almost worn out and it was impossible to put new ones in without ruining the music.

What a calamity! The mechanical bird was allowed to sing only once a year, and even that was too much. But on these occasions the Music Master made a speech filled with difficult words, proving that the bird was as good as new. And so, of course, all the courtiers said that it was as good as new.

Five years went by. Then, suddenly, a great sorrow descended on the land. Everybody loved the Emperor, but now he was sick. He was dying, people said. A new emperor had already been chosen, and people stood in the street in front of the palace and asked the Chief Imperial Gentleman-in-Waiting how their Emperor was. "Ppp!" he answered sadly, shaking his head.

The Emperor lay cold and pale in his bed. All the courtiers thought that he had already died, and they ran off to greet the new emperor. The lackeys drifted into the streets to gossip about it, and the chambermaids had a long tea party. Everywhere, in all the rooms and corridors, heavy rugs had been laid on the floor to muffle the sound of footsteps. The whole palace was as quiet as quiet could be.

But the Emperor wasn't dead. He lay stiff and pale in the magnificent bed with its long velvet curtains and heavy golden tassels. Through a high open window, the moon was shining down onto him and onto the mechanical bird.

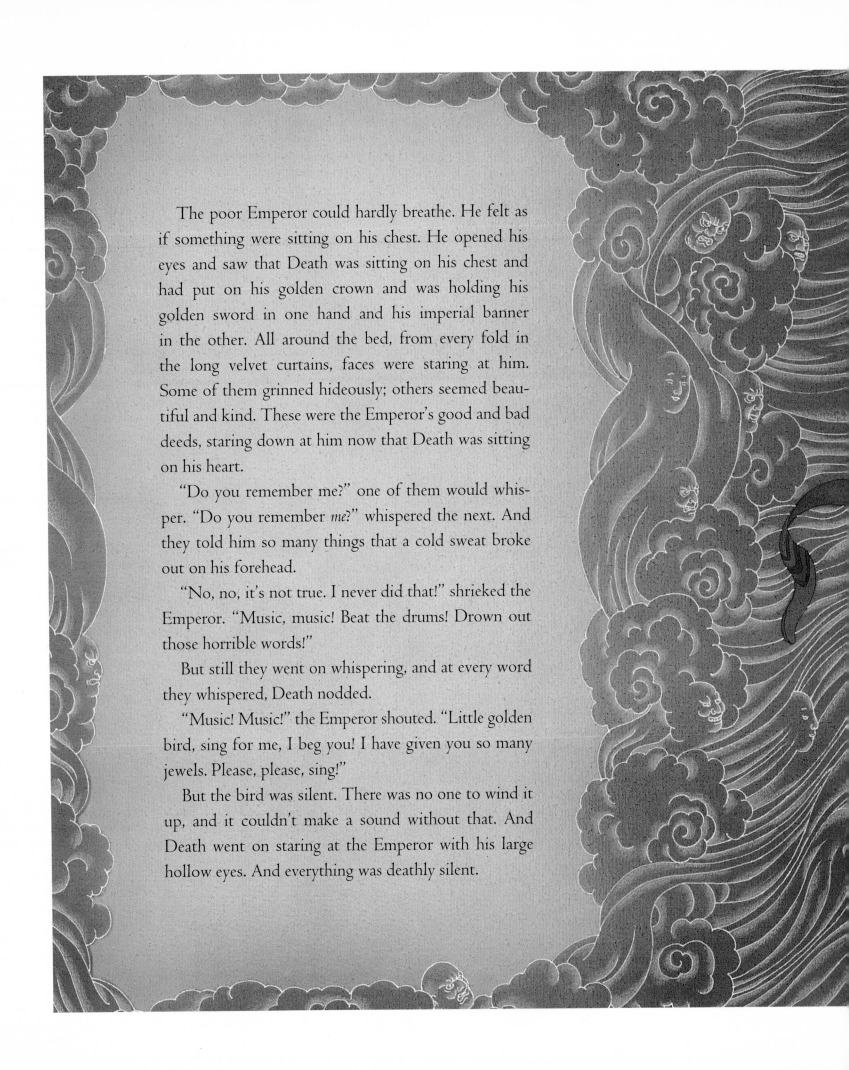

The poor Emperor could hardly breathe. He felt as if something were sitting on his chest. He opened his eyes and saw that Death was sitting on his chest and had put on his golden crown and was holding his golden sword in one hand and his imperial banner in the other. All around the bed, from every fold in the long velvet curtains, faces were staring at him. Some of them grinned hideously; others seemed beautiful and kind. These were the Emperor's good and bad deeds, staring down at him now that Death was sitting on his heart.

"Do you remember me?" one of them would whisper. "Do you remember *me?*" whispered the next. And they told him so many things that a cold sweat broke out on his forehead.

"No, no, it's not true. I never did that!" shrieked the Emperor. "Music, music! Beat the drums! Drown out those horrible words!"

But still they went on whispering, and at every word they whispered, Death nodded.

"Music! Music!" the Emperor shouted. "Little golden bird, sing for me, I beg you! I have given you so many jewels. Please, please, sing!"

But the bird was silent. There was no one to wind it up, and it couldn't make a sound without that. And Death went on staring at the Emperor with his large hollow eyes. And everything was deathly silent.

Then, all of a sudden, the whole room filled with the most beautiful singing. It was the nightingale, perched on a branch right outside the window. She had heard about the Emperor's sickness and had come to bring him hope and comfort with her song. As she sang, the ghostly faces grew fainter and fainter, the blood flowed faster and faster through the Emperor's weak body, and Death himself smiled and said, "Please go on singing, little nightingale."

"I will," she said, "if you give back the golden sword . . . if you give back the imperial banner . . . if you give back the crown."

And Death gave up each treasure for a song, and still the nightingale went on singing. She sang about the quiet graveyard where the white roses bloom, where the elder tree smells so sweet and the grass is watered by the tears of those who are left behind.

Then Death was filled with longing for his garden and floated out the window like a cold white mist.

"Thank you, thank you," said the Emperor. "You heavenly little bird, now I know who you are. I banished you from my Empire, and yet you came back to me, and you drove away those horrible visions and lifted Death from my heart. How can I ever repay you?"

"You have repaid me already," said the nightingale. "The first time I sang for you I brought tears to your eyes. I will never forget that. That is the most precious gift a singer can ever hope for. But go to sleep now and get well and strong again. I will sing you a lullaby."

And the nightingale sang, and the Emperor fell asleep, and it was the sweetest, most refreshing sleep of his life.

When the Emperor woke up, with the sun shining through the windows, he felt strong and completely healed. None of his courtiers had come yet, because they thought he was dead. But the nightingale was still singing.

"Please stay with me," said the Emperor. "You will only have to sing when you want to. And as for the mechanical bird—I will break it into a thousand pieces."

"No, don't," said the nightingale. "It has done its best; there's no reason to destroy it. I can't come to live in the palace, but let me visit when I feel like it. I will sit on this branch outside your window, and my songs will fill you with joy and peace. I will sing of those who are happy and of those who suffer, of the good and of the evil around you that you don't know about. But there are other people that I must fly to: the poor fisherman and the farmer, people who live far away from you and your court. I will come sing to you because of your heart, not your crown. But there is one thing that I want you to promise me."

"Anything!" said the Emperor, standing in the magnificent robes that he had put on, and holding the heavy golden sword to his heart.

"Just one thing: don't let anyone know that you have a little bird who tells you everything. It will be better that way."

Then the nightingale flew away.

At last the courtiers came in to pay their respects to their dead Emperor. There they all stood. And the Emperor said, "Good morning!"

A Note on This Retelling

"Nattergalen" ("The Nightingale") was written in 1844, when Hans Christian Andersen was thirty-nine years old, and published in the collection *Nye Eventyr*. The original text in Danish can be found on Det Kongelige Bibliotek [The Royal (Danish) Library] website at: www.kb.dk/elib/lit/dan/andersen.

I have called my version a retelling rather than a translation, because it adds words, it leaves other words out, it translates at an angle if that seems appropriate, it alters the structure of sentences, it even has fun amplifying the titles of the characters. A translation, it seemed to me, couldn't recreate in English the energy, wit, and charm of the original. I felt that the story would be better served by retelling it as if Andersen were writing in the English of today. So that you can have a clearer impression of what I have done, here is a literal translation of a passage from "Nattergalen" (printed in italics), followed by my version:

> *"There is supposed to be a highly remarkable bird here, called a nightingale!" said the emperor, "they say it is the most beautiful thing in my great kingdom! why haven't I been told of it!"*
> *"I have never heard of it," said the knight, "it has never been presented at Court."*
> *"I want it to come this evening and sing before me!" said the emperor. "The whole world knows what I have, and I don't know it."*
> *"I have never heard of it," said the knight, "I will look for it, I will find it!"*
> *But where was it to be found; the knight went up and down all the stairs, through rooms and passageways, no one of all he met had heard of the nightingale. And the knight ran back to the emperor, and said that it must be a fable of those who had written the book. "Your imperial Majesty should not believe everything written there! there are fabrications, and something that is called the black art."*

"It says here," said the Emperor, pointing to a page in the book, "that I have a most remarkable bird called a nightingale. She is a most extraordinary bird, it says, and the loveliest thing in all my Empire. Why haven't I been told about this?"

"It's the first time *I've* ever heard of her, Your Majesty," said the Gentleman-in-Waiting. "She has never been presented at Court."

"I *command* you to bring her here to sing for me this very evening!" said the Emperor. "Hmpf! The whole world knows about this remarkable bird of mine — except me!"

"It's the first time *I've* ever heard of her," repeated the Gentleman-in-Waiting. "I will look for her, Your Majesty, and I will find her."

Find her? But how?

The Gentleman-in-Waiting ran upstairs and downstairs, through rooms and corridors, but no one he met had ever heard of the nightingale. So he hurried back to the Emperor and said it must be a story made up by the clever people who write books. "You shouldn't believe everything you read, Your Majesty. Writers like to tell fairy tales, you know; they'll just make something up and not care whether it's true or not."

In this retelling, as I hope you can see, I have tried to be faithful to the spirit of the original, and to the spirit of the English language. — *Stephen Mitchell*

A Note on the Illustrations

The illustrator and publisher gratefully acknowledge the following invaluable source references: *The Freer Gallery of Art 1: China*, produced by Kodansha Ltd., Tokyo, Japan; *Imperial Wardrobe*, by Gary Dickinson and Linda Wrigglesworth, Ten Speed Press; *Treasures of China*, Richard Marek Publishers; *China Observed*, by Charles Meyer, Kaye and Ward London, Oxford University Press, New York; and *Five Thousand Years of Chinese Costumes*, by Zhou Xun and Gao Chunming, The Commercial Press Ltd., Hong Kong. Techniques and media used in illustrating this book include rapidograph and water-resistant acrylic ink, watercolors, gouache, and bleach.

Stephen Mitchell is a renowned writer, translator, and anthologist. His thirty books for adults and children include translations of the Gospels, Rilke, Genesis, and Job, as well as a collection of original poetry for children called *The Wishing Bone, and Other Poems*, illustrated by Tom Pohrt. His version of the *Tao Te Ching* has sold more than half a million copies. Of this retelling of Hans Christian Andersen's famous tale, he says, "*The Nightingale* is one of the most charming stories ever written. I have tried to make my version light, clear, swift, and funny."

Bagram Ibatoulline (pronounced ee-bah-too-LEEN) was born in Russia and graduated from the State Academic Institute of Arts in Moscow. He is the illustrator of the acclaimed *Crossing*, a picture book edition of a vintage poem by Philip Booth; *The Serpent Came to Gloucester* by M.T. Anderson; and *The Miraculous Journey of Edward Tulane* by Kate DiCamillo. He says of *The Nightingale*, "It has always been one of my favorite stories. While illustrating the book, I paid close attention to the tale's delicate story line and tried to portray its nature."